Grandma Lale's Tamales:
A Christmas Story

Los tamales de Abuelita Lale:
Un cuento navideño

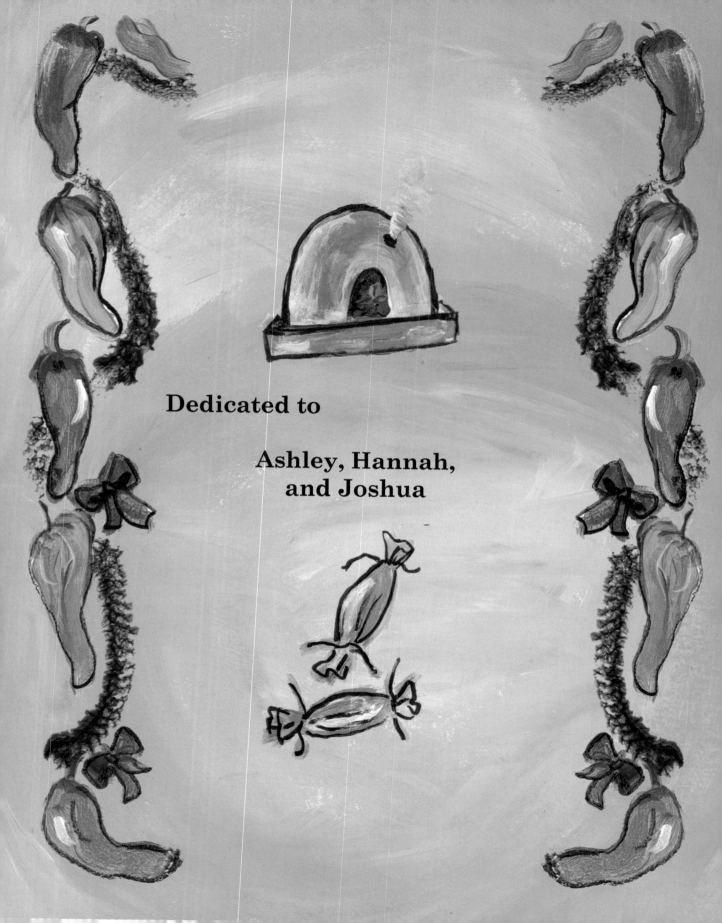

Dedicated to

Ashley, Hannah,
and Joshua

© 2014, Nasario García
Illustrations by Dolores Aragón

All rights reserved.
Rio Grande Books
Los Ranchos, New Mexico
www.LPDPress.com

Printed in the U.S.A.
Book design by Paul Rhetts

Library of Congress Cataloging-in-Publication Data

García, Nasario.
Grandma Lale's tamales : a Christmas story / Nasario Garcia ;
with illustrations by Dolores Aragón.
pages cm
Summary: In the Río Puerco valley of New Mexico, Grandma Lale teaches her grandson how to make her famous Christmas tamales. Includes recipe.
ISBN 978-1-936744-26-8 (hardcover : alk. paper)
[1. Tamales--Fiction. 2. Cooking, Mexican--Fiction. 3. Grandmothers--Fiction. 4. Christmas--Fiction. 5. Mexican Americans--Fiction. 6. New Mexico--Fiction. 7. Spanish language materials--Bilingual.] I. Aragón, Dolores, illustrator. II. Title.
PZ73.G26 2014
[E]--dc23
2014004684

Hello. My name is Junie López. I'm seven years old and I'm Grandma Lale's grandson. She was my father's mother. I grew up in the Río Puerco valley of New Mexico near the famous Cerros Cuates.* My little house was about a half a mile from the Cerros Cuates.

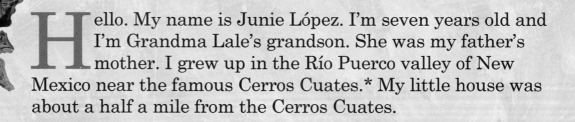

Hola. Yo me llamo Junie López. Tengo siete años de edad y soy el nieto de Abuelita Lale. Ella era la madre de mi padre. Yo me crié en el valle del Río Puerco de Nuevo México cerca de los famosos Cerros Cuates.* Mi casita estaba a una media milla de los Cerros Cuates.

* *The Cerros Cuates (Twin Peaks), Santa Clara and Guadalupe, are featured on the 2012 Centennial Stamp of New Mexico.*

This morning I did not have school, so I thought Mom would let me sleep a little late. Boy was I wrong!

"*¡Albricias, albricias!* Great news, great news! Come, *hijito*. Up, up. Today is a very special day," Mom said, her voice quivering with excitement. "And you know what that means don't you?"

"No, *amá*. I guess I forgot," I responded half asleep as I rubbed my eyes trying to wake up.

"Today's when Grandma Lale makes her famous tamales, and she wants you to help her."

"Really? I can help her?"

Esta mañana no tuve escuela, de manera que pensé que mamá me dejaría dormir un poco tarde. ¡Qué si me equivoqué!

—¡Albricias, albricias! Anda, hijito. Levántate, levántate. Hoy es un día muy especial—dijo Mamá con una voz que temblaba de emoción—. Y ya sabes lo que quiere decir eso, ¿qué no?

—No, amá. Quizás se me olvidó—respondí medio dormido mientras me refregaba los ojos tratando de despertar.

—Hoy es cuando Abuelita Lale hace sus famosos tamales, y ella quiere que tú le ayudes.

—¿De veras? ¿Puedo ayudarle?

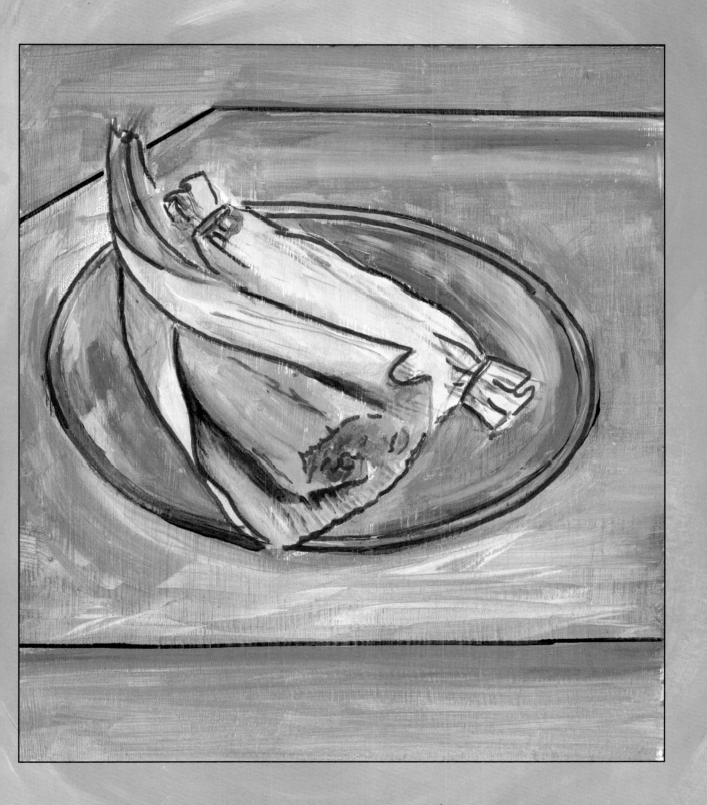

5

I gobbled down my bowl of oatmeal and started out the door to go see Grandma Lale, when suddenly I stopped in my tracks.

"*Amá*, it's snowing!"

"Yes, isn't it beautiful? It's Christmastime! I guess it snowed all night long. Before you go see your grandma, put on your *cachucha* (cap) and *manoplas* (mittens). And have your dad wrap *guangoche*, burlap around your shoes."

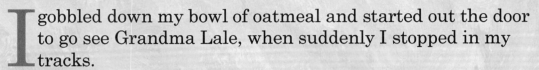

Me zampé la olla de aveno y salí a toda prisa a ver a Abuelita Lale, cuando de repente me detuve.

—Amá, ¡está nevando!

—Sí, qué bonito, ¿no? ¡Es Navidad! Creo que nevó la noche entera. Antes de que vayas a ver a tu abuelita, ponte la cachucha y las manoplas. Y que te aforre tu papá los zapatos con guangoche.

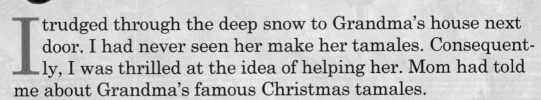

I trudged through the deep snow to Grandma's house next door. I had never seen her make her tamales. Consequently, I was thrilled at the idea of helping her. Mom had told me about Grandma's famous Christmas tamales.

"Good morning, Grandma. Mom says you're going to make your tamales today."

"Yes, *hijito*. How can I forget? *Esta noche es Nochebuena*. Tonight is Christmas Eve, and I must make my tamales today. Would you like to help me?"

"Would I!" I answered practically jumping out of my shoes. "What can I do?"

Anduve con dificultad por la alta nieve a casa de mi abuelita que estaba a un lado de la nuestra. Yo nunca la había visto hacer sus tamales, así que estaba todo emocionado en poder ayudarle. Mamá me había contado de los famosos tamales navideños de mi abuelita.

—Buenos días le dé Dios, Abuelita. Mamá me dice que usted va a hacer sus tamales hoy.

—Sí, hijito. ¿Cómo se me puede olvidar? Esta noche es Nochebuena, y tengo que hacer mis tamales hoy. ¿Te gustaría ayudarme?

—¡Qué si me gustaría!—contesté casi dando saltos—. ¿En qué puedo ayudarle?

"The first thing we have to do is to go to the shed."

"And what are we going to do there?"

"Come. I'll show you," and we walked down to the shed a short distance from Grandma's house. She opened the squeaky wooden door and entered. I stood at the entrance with the door ajar so what little daylight was available could shine in.

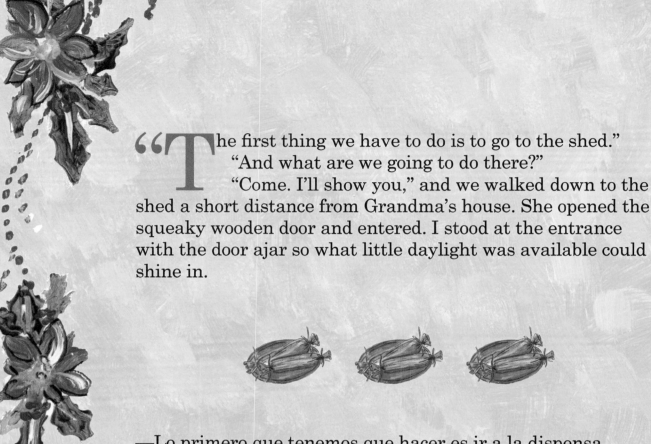

—Lo primero que tenemos que hacer es ir a la dispensa.

—¿Y qué vamos a hacer allí?

—Ven. Ya verás—y fuimos andando cuesta abajo a la dispensa a una corta distancia de la casa de mi abuelita. Abrió la puerta rechinante de madera y entró. Yo me quedé parado a la puerta con la puerta entreabierta para que entrara la poca de luz que había.

11

"There he is!" and she pointed to a hog's head hanging from a wooden beam or *viga*. I wasn't surprised, or scared; this scene was part of ranch life for little boys like me. "That's my friend Tito!" Grandma added. "Do you remember him from last month's *matanza*?"

"Yes, yes, Grandma," I stammered. "But why is he wearing one of Grandpa's old cowboy hats?"

"Ah, *hijito*. That cowboy hat is to keep his head warm in the winter. He must also look elegant."

—¡Ahi lo tienes!—y apuntó a una cabeza de marrano que estaba colgada de una viga. No me quedé sorprendido ni asustado; esta escena era parte de la vida en el rancho para muchachitos como yo—. ¡Ése es mi amigo Tito!—añadió mi abuelita—. ¿Te acuerdas de él y la matanza del mes pasado?

—Sí, sí, Abuelita—tartamudeé—. ¿Pero por qué tiene puesto un sombrero viejo de mi abuelito?

—Ah, hijito. Ese sombrero vaquero es para que tenga la cabeza calentita en el invierno. También ha de verse pantera.

Grandma Lale was a serious person, but from time to time she could surprise you with her sense of humor. She brought the pig's head down from the *viga* and carefully carried it in her arms back to her house. The wood stove was nice and warm when we walked in the kitchen.

"Here," and she removed the hat from Tito and put it on me. "That's to show him respect," and she smiled. "Now, open the stove oven," and she put Tito inside.

Abuelita Lale era una persona seria, pero de vez en cuando podía sorprenderle a uno con su sentido de humor. Ella bajó la cabeza del marrano de la viga y la llevó en brazos a su casa. La estufa de leña estaba bien calentita cuando entramos en la cocina.

—Toma—y le quitó el sombrero a Tito y me lo puso a mí—. Eso es pa demostrarle respeto a él—y se sonrió ella—. Ahora bien, abre el horno de la estufa—y puso a Tito dentro.

14

"When will the pig be done, Grandma?"

"Oh, it will take a little while, but don't call him a pig. You'll hurt his feelings. Remember, his name is Tito, OK?"

"And why did you name him Tito?"

"Tito comes from Manuelito; it means peace in Spanish. And Christmas is the season of peace on Earth. All right, we have to get several things ready before making the tamales."

"Like what, Grandma?"

—¿Cuándo estará listo el marrano, Abuelita?

—Oh, tardará un buen rato, pero no le llames marrano. Le puedes herir sus sentimientos. Acuérdate que se llama Tito. ¿De acuerdo?

—¿Y por qué le puso el nombre Tito?

—Tito viene de Manuelito; quiere decir paz. Y Navidad es la temporada de paz en este mundo. Bueno, tenemos que alistar varias cosas antes de hacer los tamales.

—¿Cómo qué, Abuelita?

"Well, besides the pig, oops, I meant to say Tito, we need a large bowl, a deep pot, a steamer, the *masa* (corn paste), a tablespoon, corn husks, red chile, and a couple of cloves of garlic for the chile. OK, let's get to work."

Grandma filled the bowl with *nixtamal*—the corn paste for the tamales. She had ground the corn on a *metate*, a grinding stone.

"All right. Get me some water in that pitcher that's on top of the small table. We're going to knead the *masa*."

—Pues bien. Además del marrano, ¡ay caray!, quise decir Tito, necesitamos una olla grande, una bandeja honda, una olla de estofar, la masa de maíz, una cuchara, hojas de maíz, chile colorado, y unos dos dientes de ajo para el chile. Bueno, a trabajar.

Mi abuelita llenó la olla con nixtamal—la masa para los tamales. Ella había machacado el maíz en un metate.

—Bueno. Traeme agua en ese pichel que está arriba de esa mesita. Vamos a hacer la masa.

I had helped Mom make tortillas many times, but the masa for the tamales had a different feel as I stuck my hands in the bowl. It was grainy and felt like sand between my fingers. Grandma and I took turns kneading the paste-like *masa* until we had a big ball which she covered with a dishtowel to keep it from getting dry.

"Now it's time to visit our friend Tito," Grandma Lale said, and she opened the stove oven. "Sure enough! He'll be ready in no time at all."

Yo le había ayudado a mamá muchas veces hacer tortillas de harina, pero la masa para los tamales tenía un toque diferente cuando metí las manos en la olla. La masa estaba granosa y se sentía como arena entre los dedos. Primero amasaba mi abuelita y luego yo hasta que ya teníamos una bola grande de masa, la cual ella tapó con un trapo para que no se secara.

—Ahora es hora de visitar a nuestro amigo Tito—dijo Abuelita Lale, y abrió el horno de la estufa—. ¡Dicho y hecho! Falta poco pa que esté listo.

17

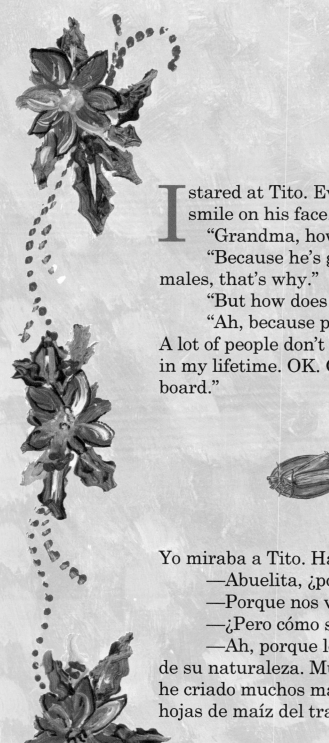

I stared at Tito. Even without his hat, he had a kind of a smile on his face.

"Grandma, how come Tito looks so happy?"

"Because he's going to bring us happiness with the tamales, that's why."

"But how does he know he's going to make us happy?"

"Ah, because pigs are smart; that's part of their nature. A lot of people don't know that, but I do. I've raised many pigs in my lifetime. OK. Go get me the corn husks from the cupboard."

Yo miraba a Tito. Hasta sin sombrero, tenía una sonrisita.

—Abuelita, ¿por qué Tito se ve tan alegre?

—Porque nos va a alegrar el corazón con los tamales.

—¿Pero cómo sabe que nos va a alegrar?

—Ah, porque los marranos son inteligentes. Es parte de su naturaleza. Mucha gente no sabe eso, pero yo sí sé. Yo he criado muchos marranos en mi vida. Bueno. Ve traeme las hojas de maíz del trastero.

19

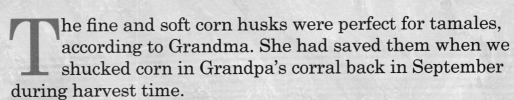

The fine and soft corn husks were perfect for tamales, according to Grandma. She had saved them when we shucked corn in Grandpa's corral back in September during harvest time.

"Tito must be ready by now. Let's take him out of his hiding place," Grandma Lale said with a slight grin.

She grabbed a pair of Grandpa Lolo's canvas gloves, opened the hot oven, took out the tin platter with Tito on it, and placed both on a small table on the portal.

Según mi abuelita, las hojas delgaditas y blanditas de maíz eran perfectas para tamales. Ella las había guardado cuando deshojamos maíz en el corral de mi abuelito en septiembre durante la cosecha.

—Tito ya debe de estar listo. Vamos a sacarlo de su escondite—dijo Abuelita Lale con una sonrisita.

Agarró un par de guantes de lona de Abuelito Lolo, abrió el horno que estaba caliente, sacó la bandeja con Tito en ella, y la puso sobre una mesita en el portal.

"While Tito's cooling off," Grandma said, "let's make the red chile. Afterwards, you and I can start the fire in the adobe *horno* for the tamales."

"But aren't you going to cook the tamales on the wood stove, Grandma?"

"No, *hijito*. The meat is already cooked, and the chile will also be ready. The only thing left is the *masa*. And so, we'll steam the tamales in the adobe *horno*; that's how we'll cook the *masa*."

"But why the *horno*, Grandma?"

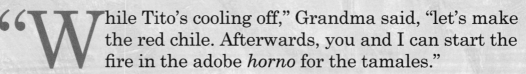

—Mientras Tito se está enfriando—dijo mi abuelita— vamos a preparar el chile. Después podemos prender tú y yo la lumbre en el horno de adobe para los tamales.

—Pero Abuelita, ¿que no va a cocinar los tamales en la estufa de leña?

—No, hijito. La carne ya está cocinada, y el chile también estará listo. Lo único que falta es la masa. Así que vamos a cocer los tamales al vapor en el horno; es así cómo coceremos la masa.

—¿Pero por qué en el horno, Abuelita?

"Ah, funny you should ask! Because by steaming the tamales in the *horno*, they will have a *piñón* smoked flavor to them. That's the beauty of burning *piñón* wood. *Piñón* flavored tamales are your grandma's specialty. I learned that from my grandma in Corrales northwest of Albuquerque when I was a little girl."

We went outside to the *horno* next to the shed. Grandma Lale grabbed a few *piñón* logs and stacked them standing one by one inside the *horno* like a tepee.

To quick start the fire, she placed a long piece of *ocote*, torch pine in the middle of the logs and lit a match to it. The wood didn't take long to burn brightly, nor for smoke to start bellowing through the top opening of the *horno*.

—¡Ah, cosa curiosa que me preguntes! Porque cocinando los tamales al vapor en el horno, tendrán un sabor ahumado a piñón. Ésa es la belleza de la leña de piñón. Los tamales a sabor de piñón son la especialidad de tu abuelita. Yo aprendí a hacerlos de mi abuelita en Corrales al noroeste de Alburquerque cuando yo era niña.

Salimos para fuera a donde estaba el horno a un lado de la dispensa. Abuelita Lale agarró unos leños de piñón y los puso uno por uno como un tepee, dentro del horno.

Para prender la lumbre bien rápido, ella puso un pedazo largo de ocote en medio de los leños y lo prendió con un fósforo. No tardó mucho la leña en arder brillante. Tampoco tardó en escaparse el humo por el copete del horno.

24

"Ready, *hijito*? Now comes the fun part. Follow me," and Abuelita Lale walked slowly through the deep snow back to the portal. I wondered for a split second what she was going to do. "Remember, 'whatever a child hears in the corral, he repeats it on the portal.'"

I had heard her *dicho*, folk saying before; it meant that children learned from their elders by listening and observing.

"And something else," Grandma added, "a lot of people don't know this, but the best part of the hog and perfect for making tamales is the meat that comes from the head and jaws. The meat is tender and delicious. Here, try some," and Grandma Lale handed me a small piece. Boy was it tasty!

—¿Listo, hijito? Ahora viene lo divertido. Sígueme—y se fue andando Abuelita Lale a un paso lento por toda la nieve hasta llegar al portal. Por un breve momento no supe qué iba a hacer ella—. Acuérdate, 'lo que un niño oye en el corral, lo repite en el portal.'

Yo había oído su dicho antes. Quería decir que los hijos escuchando y observando aprendían de los mayores.

—Y una cosa más—añadió mi abuelita—, muncha gente no sabe esto, pero lo mejor del marrano y perfecto pa hacer tamales es la carne que viene de la cabeza y de las mandíbulas. La carne es tiernita y sabrosa. Toma, pruébala—y me dio un pedacito. ¡Qué si estaba sabrosa!

By the time she finished pulling the meat, she had a bowl full, enough meat for about one dozen tamales, according to Grandma. She took the meat and placed it next to the pan of water that was by the chile, *masa*, and corn husks.

"Grandma, what's the water for?"

"The warm water is to dip the corn husks so they are soft. In that way, it's easier to fold them into tamales. OK. We are now ready for the tamales," Grandma said as she rubbed her hands together ready for action. "Watch carefully how I make the first *tamal*. Then you can help me with the rest."

Para cuando ella acabó de arrancar la carne, ya tenía una olla llena, bastante carne, según mi abuelita, para una docena de tamales. Cogió la carne y la puso junto a la bandeja de agua que estaba al lado del chile, de la masa, y de las hojas de maíz.

—Abuelita, ¿pa qué es l'agua?

—L' agua tibia es pa meter la hojas de maíz pa que estén blanditas. Asina se doblan más fácil al hacer los tamales. Bueno. Ya estamos listos pa los tamales—dijo mi abuelita frotándose las manos, lista para trabajar—. Mira con cuidado cómo es que hago el primer tamal. Luego me puedes ayudar con los demás.

27

I watched Grandma Lale very carefully. She was just as meticulous in making a *tamal* as she was in building the stack of wood inside the *horno*. First, she placed two corn husks flat on the table, one interfaced with the other. Next she spread the *masa* with her right hand on the corn husks, followed by a few strands of meat and two or three table-spoons of red chile. Now it was time to fold the corn husks one overlapping the other. Once she did that, she tied the corn husks at each end with a small piece of wet corn husk. Just like that the *tamal* was done! I could tell that Grandma Lale was not only proud, but she was also a master at making tamales.

"There you have it! How do you like that? That's the first *tamal*. Now it's your turn."

Yo observé a Abuelita Lale con mucho cuidado. Ella era tan cuidadosa en hacer un tamal, como lo era al construir el tepee de leña en el horno de adobe. Primero puso dos hojas abiertas de maíz en la mesa, una entrelazada con la otra. Después con la mano derecha cubrió las hojas de masa, junto con unas hebras de carne y dos o tres cucharadas de chile colorado. Ahora había llegado el momento de doblar las hojas de maíz, una hoja medio cubierta sobre la otra. Al hacer eso, ató las hojas en cada orilla con un pedacito de hoja mojada. ¡En un decir amén el tamal estaba hecho! Se notaba que Abuelita Lale no solamente se sentía orgullosa sino que también era una maestra para hacer tamales.

—¡Ahi lo tienes! ¿Qué te parece? Ése es el primer tamal. Ahora te toca a ti.

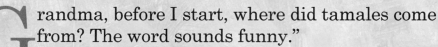

"Grandma, before I start, where did tamales come from? The word sounds funny."

"Good question. My grandma in Corrales once told me that tamales are an Indian food that came from Mexico a long time ago. We have been enjoying them here in New Mexico ever since. All right, it's your turn to make a *tamal*."

Step by step, I repeated what Grandma Lale had shown me. She watched to make sure I did it right. In the process, her words of wisdom buzzed in my head: *"Whatever a child hears in the corral, he repeats it on the portal."*

Displaying a joyous smile, Grandma Lale approved of my first-ever *tamal*.

—Abuelita, antes que comience yo, ¿de dónde vinieron los tamales? La palabra me suena un poco extraño.

—Buena pregunta. Mi abuelita en Corrales me dijo una vez que los tamales son una comida indígena que vino de México hace munchos años. Desde ese entonces, los hemos venido saboreando aquí en Nuevo México. Bueno, te toca a ti hacer un tamal.

Paso por paso, repetí lo que mi Abuelita Lale me había enseñado. Ella me observaba para estar segura que yo hacía todo bien. En el proceso, sus palabras de sabiduría me zumbaban en la cabeza, *"Lo que un niño oye en el corral, lo repite en el portal."*

Con una risita de alegría, Abuelita Lale aplaudió mi primer merito tamal.

31

"Wonderful! You're a master *tamal*-maker already!" Grandma exclaimed, and we continued making the rest of the tamales.

"By now the *horno* must be ready," Grandma Lale said, and we went to see.

She grabbed a long metal shovel that was near the *horno* and removed the hot coals from inside and placed them in a tin bucket. To make sure the *horno* wasn't too hot for the tamales, Grandma took a small piece of sheep's wool from her apron pocket, pinned it to the tip of a long piece of baling wire, and tested the temperature inside the adobe oven.

¡Qué maravilla! ¡Ya eres un tamalero de primera categoría!— exclamó mi abuelita, y continuamos haciendo el resto de los tamales.

—Yo creo que el horno de adobe ya debe de estar listo— dijo Abuelita Lale, y fuimos a ver.

Agarró una pala larga de metal que estaba cerca del horno y sacó las brasas calientes de dentro del horno y las echó en una cubeta de hojalata. Para estar segura que el horno no estuviera muy caliente, Abuelita Lale sacó un pedacito de lana de borrega de su delantal, la puso en la punta de un alambre largo de empacar, y probó la temperatura del horno.

33

"*Mira*, look," Grandma said. "If the wool turns black, the *horno* is too hot, but if the wool turns light brown like it is now, the temperature is just right for steaming the tamales."

I listened to Grandma and watched every move she made. She filled the deep-round tin pot half-full of water and then put the steamer inside the pot. Next Grandma Lale grabbed a wooden shovel that she used for baking loaves of bread in the *horno* and gently pushed the tin pot inside the horno to steam the tamales. The tamales were on top of the steamer.

—Mira—dijo mi abuelita—. Si la lana se vuelve negra, el horno está demasiado caliente, pero si la lana se vuelve color acafetado como está ahora, la temperatura está perfecta para cocer los tamales al vapor.

Yo escuchaba a mi abuelita y observaba cada una de sus acciones. Medio llenó de agua la olla honda y redonda de estaño y luego puso la olla de estofar dentro de la olla de estaño. Después Abuelita Lale agarró una pala de madera que usaba para hacer sus tortas de pan en el horno, y empujó poco a poquito la olla de estaño hacia adentro del horno para cocer los tamales al vapor. Los tamales estaban encima de la olla de estofar.

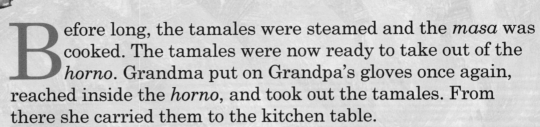

Before long, the tamales were steamed and the *masa* was cooked. The tamales were now ready to take out of the *horno*. Grandma put on Grandpa's gloves once again, reached inside the *horno*, and took out the tamales. From there she carried them to the kitchen table.

"But when do we get to taste one, Grandma?" I asked somewhat eagerly.

"Ah, my anxious little beaver! That's a surprise and part of the Christmas spirit. You'll just have to wait. For now, it's time for you to go eat lunch and take your *siesta*, so scoot on home. See you tonight for *La Misa del Gallo*, Midnight Mass."

No tardó mucho en cocerse al vapor los tamales y la masa. Los tamales ahora estaban listos para sacarlos del horno. Abuelita Lale se volvió a poner los guantes de mi abuelito, metió las manos en el horno, y sacó los tamales. De allí los llevó a la mesa en la cocina.

—¿Pero cuándo podemos probar uno, Abuelita?—le pregunté un poco intranquilo.

—¡Ah niño ansioso! Ésa es una sorpresa y parte del espíritu navideño. Tendrás que esperarte. Por ahora, es hora de que te vayas a comer y a dormir la siesta, así que chalequéale a casa. Nos vemos esta noche pa la Misa del Gallo.

Late that night Grandpa Lolo harnessed his team of horses and hitched them to the wagon. Mom and Dad rode on their horse wagon, but Grandma Lale asked me to go with her and Grandpa to our *placita*, village. I wondered why? I thought perhaps that it had something to do with the tamales, but I was wrong. Instead, she wanted me to join her and her children's choir for rehearsal before Midnight Mass started. I was so thrilled about singing in the choir for the first time that I totally forgot about the tamales.

The *Virgen de Guadalupe* Church in our village was across the Río Puerco about two miles from our *ranchito*. As we reached the river, I saw a string of bright lights glowing in the *placita*.

Ya tarde esa noche Abuelito Lolo le puso las guarniciones a su tiro de caballos y prendió los caballos al carro de caballos. Mamá y Papá fueron en su carro de caballos, pero Abuelita Lale me convidó a que fuera con ella y mi abuelito a la placita. Me preguntaba que si por qué. Yo pensaba que tal vez tuviera algo que ver con los tamales, pero me equivoqué. Ella quería que yo la acompañara a ella y a su coro de niños para un ensayo antes de que empezara La Misa del Gallo. Yo estaba tan excitado de cantar en el coro por primera vez que me olvidé por completo de los tamales.

La iglesia de la Virgen de Guadalupe en nuestra placita estaba al otro lado del Río Puerco a unas dos millas de nuestro ranchito. Al acercarnos al río, vi un chorro de luces relumbrantes en la placita.

"Look, Grandma! What are those lights?" I asked all excited.

"*Hijito*, those are *luminarios*."

"And what are *luminarios*?"

"They are small bonfires to help guide the people to the church on Christmas Eve to celebrate the *Misa del Gallo* in honor of the birth of the Baby Jesus. Legend has it that a rooster crowed the night Jesus was born. That's why it's called *Misa del Gallo*. And the *luminarios* will light up the *placita* until Midnight Mass is over."

—¡Mire, Abuelita! ¿Qué son aquellas luces?—le pregunté todo excitado.

—Hijito, esas luces son luminarios.

—¿Y qué son luminarios?

—Son pequeñas hogueras para guiar a la gente a la iglesia durante Nochebuena para celebrar la Misa del Gallo en honor del nacimiento de nuestro Niño Jesús. Se dice que un gallo cantó la noche en que nació Jesucristo. Es por eso que se llama La Misa del Gallo. Y los luminarios alumbrarán la placita hasta cuando termine la Misa del Gallo.

When we got to the church, two rows of *luminarios* burned brightly up and down the snowy entrance to the church. The small stacks of juniper wood crackled and popped as Grandma and I went inside to join the young boys and girls from our *placita* to sing *villancicos*, Christmas carols. Mom told me later that Grandma had been singing Christmas songs for several years.

By the time the priest came out from the sacristy to start the Mass, the church was packed with people of all ages: grownups, young people, little kids, and babies in their mothers' arms. The altar was also glowing with tall white wax candles. The mood was festive, and the *villancicos* were beautiful.

Cuando llegamos a la iglesia, ardían dos carreras de luminarios, una en cada lado de la entrada. Las pequeñas pilas de leña de piñón chisporroteaban y explotaban al entrar yo y mi Abuelita Lale para reunirnos con los niños y niñas de nuestra placita para cantar villancicos. Mamá me dijo más tarde que mi abuelita ya llevaba varios años cantando villancicos.

Ya para cuando el padre salió de la sacristía para empezar la misa, la iglesia estaba llenita de gente: adultos, jóvenes, niños, y criaturas en brazos de las mamás. El altar también brillaba con velas altas y blancas, de cera. Reinaba un ambiente alegre, y los villancicos eran preciosos.

But for me the best part of the Mass was to hear Grandma Lale's solo singing of *Noche de Paz*, Silent Night. Her melodic voice was truly heavenly and peaceful. I thought of what she had told me before about the name Tito symbolizing peace. I felt so proud of my grandma and glad she had invited me to be a part of her choir.

Pero para mí lo mejor de la misa fue oír a mi Abuelita Lale cantar Noche de Paz. Su canto fue algo divino y sereno. Pensé en lo que me había dicho antes del nombre Tito que simboliza paz. Me sentí tan orgulloso de mi abuelita y me dio gusto por haberme invitado ella a formar parte de su coro.

Once the *Misa del Gallo* was over, Grandma Lale, Mom, and I went up to the altar to view the *Nacimiento*, the Nativity Scene. The Baby Jesus was in a small straw manger on a mound of dirt on the adobe floor. There were several large *yeso* animals surrounding the Baby Jesus: a donkey, a sheep, a cow, and, of course, a rooster. The cow's breath, according to Grandma Lale, provided warmth to the Baby Jesus after He was born. I recognized the *Nacimiento*; it was the same one that Grandma set up in her bedroom.

Habiéndose terminado la Misa del Gallo, yo, Abuelita Lale, y mamá nos acercamos al altar a ver el Nacimiento. El Santo Niño estaba en un pequeño pesebre de paja arriba de una pila de tierra en el suelo que también era de tierra. Alrededor del Niño Jesús había varios animales de yeso, entre ellos un burrito, una oveja, una vaca, y un gallo, por supuesto. El resuello de la vaca, según mi Abuelita Lale, le consagró calor al Niño Jesús después que nació. Yo reconocí el Nacimiento; era el mismo que ponía mi abuelita en su recámara.

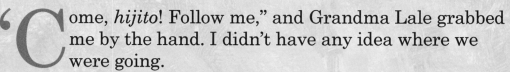

"Come, *hijito*! Follow me," and Grandma Lale grabbed me by the hand. I didn't have any idea where we were going.

We walked into the sacristy. The first thing I noticed was a wooden table with Grandma's white enameled tin plates, knives, forks, cups, and glasses that she used whenever guests came to her home. The table was set for eating. As I glanced around I saw on top of the potbelly stove the pot that Grandma had used to steam the tamales. Now, I was really curious.

"All right, *hijito*, put a *leño*, a piece of wood, in the stove to make sure the stove is hot. We're going to heat up the tamales so we can eat." Grandma said.

—Ven, hijito. Vente conmigo—y Abuelita Lale me agarró de la mano. No tuve ni la menor idea a dónde íbamos.

Entramos en la sacristía. Lo primero que vi fue una mesa de madera con los platos blancos de estaño de mi abuelita junto con cuchillos, tenedores, tazas, y vasos que usaba ella cuando venían huéspedes a su casa. La mesa estaba puesta para comer. Al dar yo un vistazo vi encima del fogoncito la olla que había usado mi abuelita para cocer los tamales al vapor. Ahora sí que me moría de curiosidad.

—Bueno, hijito, ponle un leño al fogoncito para que esté caliente. Vamos a calentar los tamales para comer—dijo mi abuelita.

Grandma Lale didn't take long to warm up the tamales. By then, the priest, Grandpa Lolo, Mom, and Dad had come into the sacristy.

"*Arrímense, arrímense*, have a sit, have a sit," Grandma said.

The mystery of when and where we would eat her tamales was no longer in doubt, but after we all sat down at the table and the priest blessed the tamales, something else was bothering me. I just had to get it off my chest.

"Grandma, you have always told your grandchildren not to eat pork at night because if we did, a pig would rumble and tumble in our tummies and make us sick."

Abuelita Lale tardó poco en calentar los tamales. Para ese entonces, el cura, Abuelito Lolo, mamá y papá habían entrado en la sacristía.

—Arrímense, arrímense a la mesa—dijo mi abuelita.

El misterio de cuándo y dónde comeríamos sus tamales jamás estaba en dudas, pero después que nos sentamos todos a la mesa y el padre bendijo los tamales, algo más me estaba molestando. Yo simplemente tenía que echarlo fuera.

—Abuelita, usted siempre les ha dicho a sus nietos que no coman carne de marrano por la noche porque si no, el marrano podía hacer ruidos en la panza y enfermarnos.

"You're right, *hijito*, but that's only true if you eat pork for supper. It's now past midnight and a perfect time to eat tamales. Besides, Tito would never give you a tummy ache," Grandma Lale added with a wink.

Before I took a bite of my tamal, I looked at the priest at the head of the table. Perspiration was dripping down his face, and it wasn't because the room was too hot. It had to be the spicy chile.

As I unfolded the corn husks, I took a bite of my first *tamal*. It was fire!

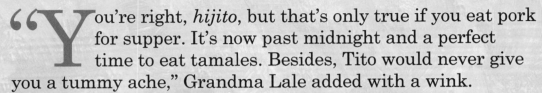

—Tienes razón, hijito, pero eso es si comen carne de marrano pa la cena. Ahora ya pasa de la medianoche y es el tiempo ideal pa comer tamales. No sólo eso, Tito jamás te daría dolor de panza—dijo Abuelita Lale con un guiño.

Antes que tomara un bocado de mi tamal, miré al padre al frente de la mesa. Le escurría sudor por la cara, y no era porque el cuarto estaba demasiado caliente. Tenía que ser el chile quemoso.

Al desdoblar yo las hojas de maíz, tomé mi primer bocado del tamal. ¡Era lumbre!

"Grandma, the chile's too hot! I can't eat my tamales."

"Ah, don't worry. I have two extras without chile just for you."

"I thought we only made twelve tamales. Who gets the two extras?"

"The two extras are for Father Nieto to take with him back to Jémez Springs."

"Thank you *hermana*, my sister," the priest said. "And by the way, these tamales are truly delicious. They're good enough to lick one's fingers. They have a smoked flavor to them that is out of this world. I had never in my life tasted tamales like these. No wonder people talk about your tamales. What's your secret?"

—Abuelita, ¡el chile está muy quemoso! No me puedo comer los tamales.

—Ah, no te apenes. Me sobran dos sin chile. Son sólo pa ti.

—Yo creí que solamente habíamos hecho doce tamales. ¿A quién le tocan los dos extras?

—Los dos que sobran son pa que el Padre Nieto se los lleve consigo a Jémez Springs.

—Gracias, hermana—dijo el padre—. A propósito, estos tamales están verdaderamente sabrosos. Son para chuparse uno los dedos. Tienen un sabor ahumado que es divino. Jamás en la vida había comido tamales como éstos. Con razón habla la gente de sus tamales. ¿Cuál es su secreto?

"Ah, *padre*. My sins I will confess, but the secret to my tamales I cannot reveal," and Grandma Lale winked at me while Grandpa, Mom, and Dad enjoyed their tamales.

"Ah, *hermana*, you have a good sense of humor."

"But there is something I can tell you, *padre*" Grandma added.

"And what's that?" exclaimed the padre.

"These were my last Christmas tamales. I will never make them again."

"Oh, no! That can't be! People throughout the entire Río Puerco valley, including folks back at Jémez Springs, know the reputation your Christmas tamales enjoy."

—Ah, padre. Confesaré mis pecados, pero el secreto de mis tamales no lo puedo divulgar—y me hizo un guiño Abuelita Lale mientras mi abuelito, mamá, y papá saboreaban sus tamales.

—Ah, hermana, usted tiene un buen sentido de humor.

—Pero hay algo que sí le puedo decir, padre—añadió mi abuelita.

—¿Y qué es eso?—exclamó el padre.

—Éstos eran mis últimos tamales navideños. Jamás los volveré a hacer.

—¡Oh, no! ¡No puede ser! La gente por todo el valle del Río Puerco, inclusive la de Jémez Springs, sabe de la fama que tienen sus deliciosos tamales navideños.

"Well, Father, it gives me great pleasure to know that my tamales are well known beyond my *placita*. I'll always treasure the wonderful memories, but my husband and I are getting old. Come fall we must give up ranch life and move to Albuquerque where our sons and daughters can look after us. Because listen Father," and Grandma paused for a brief moment, 'On this Earth old age is like flees on an old dog; it can't escape a single illness.'"

—Pues padre, me da muncho gusto saber que mis tamales se conocen más allá de mi placita. Siempre guardaré los buenos recuerdos, pero mi esposo y yo nos estamos haciendo viejos. Al llegarse el otoño hay que abandonar la vida del rancho y mudarnos a Alburquerque donde nos podrán cuidar nuestros hijos. Porque mire padre—y pausó mi abuelita por un breve momento—, "En este mundo no hay perro viejo que no se le prendan las pulgas."

The priest lowered his head upon hearing Grandma Lale's bittersweet words. There was nothing to say. His facial expression said it all.

"Grandma, is it really true that these were your last tamales, ever?" I asked while the only noise that could be heard at that given moment was Mom clearing the table.

"That's right, *hijito*. That's why I wanted you to help me so you'd have some good *recuerdos*, memories about my tamales. And remember," she cautioned me as we left the church before heading home in the cold wee hours of the morning, 'my tamales are like the leaves on an autumn tree; they couldn't last forever.' *Hijito*, everything on this precious Earth has to end. That's God's law."

El padre agachó la cabeza al oír las palabras agridulces de Abuelita Lale. Pues no quedaba nada que decir. Su cara lo decía todo.

—Abuelita, ¿es verdad que usted jamás volverá a hacer sus tamales?—le pregunté mientras el único ruido que se oía en aquel momento era mamá que levantaba la mesa.

—Es cierto, hijito. Por eso quería que me ayudaras pa que tuvieras unos buenos recuerdos de mis tamales. Y acuérdate—me advirtió al dejar nosotros la iglesia antes de irnos a casa en aquellas horas congeladas de la madrugada—, mis tamales son como las hojas de un árbol en otoño; no podían durar pa siempre. Hijito, todo en este mundo precioso tiene su fin. Ésa es la ley de Dios.

Typical Río Puerco Valley Recipe for Tamales

*R*ecipes for making tamales in New Mexico are usually quite simple, but they may vary from one household to another. Here is a recipe that Grandma Lale used at Christmastime.

Pork—preferably from hog's head and jaws, but shoulder or loin is suitable.
Chile—handmade red chile sauce (*chile caribe*) or prepared using chile powder.
Dough—*masa* made from *nixtamal*, lime water hominy.
Garlic—one or more cloves depending on the amount of chile sauce.
Water—needed for chile sauce, to knead the dough, and to soften corn husks.
Salt—the meat and dough naturally contain salt so adding salt for seasoning was optional.
Corn husks—though not ingredients as such, they comprise an integral part of the tamal-making process; how many depended on the number of tamales. Two corn husks are needed per tamal.

Once the pork is cooked, usually in a stove oven, it should be shredded into small pieces; this makes it easier when spreading on the *masa*. The old-fashioned chile sauce called *chile caribe*, made by hand, was the women's task. They washed and roasted the chile pods in the stove oven. Then they removed the stems, white veins and seeds. Next the pods were put in a pan with boiling water until it cooled before women kneaded the pods until the pulp was separated from the chile skins. Nowadays blenders are used for the task; either that or chile powder is used in making the sauce. As for the *masa*, dough, it comes from *nixtamal*, corn boiled in lime water and then ground in a *metate* (see vocabulary) before adding water to knead the *masa* for the tamales. Special corn husks were set aside when shucking corn; they were usually thinner than ordinary corn husks and perfect for folding into tamales after being dipped in warm water. A finely chopped clove of garlic (*diente de ajo*) generally sufficed. Water for the chile sauce, kneading the dough, and softening the corn husks was always present.

When the forgoing preparations were ready, putting the tamales together was the last step before they were steamed and ready to eat. Two corn husks were dipped in warm water for softening. Then a thin layer of *masa* was spread by hand on two flat inter-faced corn husks before adding a modest amount of meat on top as well as chile sauce without saturating the *masa* (Tamales without chile were also made for children who didn't eat chile.). Lastly, the two interfaced corn husks were folded before tying both ends with tiny strands of moist corn husk. This process continued until all the desired tamales were prepared whereupon they were steamed in an adobe oven as explained in the story, or by using a double-boiler—the modern way.

Note: *Long ago women in Hispanic villages never measured the amount of ingredients in cooking or baking. They did everything by instinct and never failed to put delicious food or pastries on the table.*

Glosario/Glossary

Terms once popular in my family and among my relatives and residents throughout the Río Puerco valley where I grew up.

ahi	*Ahi* was once used by Hispanic old-timers of northern New Mexico and southern Colorado instead of *ahí*.
acafetado	Brownish or light brown; used instead of *marrón claro*.
albricias	An expression of surprise to convey good news; usually repeated twice.
amá	A kid's way of addressing his mother rather than the standard *mamá*.
asina	An archaic form of *así* although it along with other archaisms have practically disappeared from today's lexicon.
aveno	The masculine form instead of *avena* was prevalent among Río Puerco valley residents.
buenos días le dé Dios	Until forty to fifty years ago this expression was common among young and old people when greeting each other in the morning instead of using the traditional *Buenos días* for Good Morning. It was also a sign of respect especially when a young person greeted an elder. Interestingly, the phrase is still heard in parts of rural Spain.
cachucha	A cap with earflaps; sometimes made of leather.
chalequear	Used among residents in my Río Puerco valley; it meant several things: to scoot, get the led out, as well as to fork out money.
chopos	Galoshes: a pair of waterproof shoes, often made of rubber, worn over other shoes as protection against rain or snow; also house slippers.
dispensa	A storage shed made of mud adobes to store perishables during hot weather as well as meat and canned fruits and vegetables during the winter. *Despensa* is the more standard spelling.
guangoche	Many people in the Río Puerco valley didn't have regular galoshes. We used burlap (*guangoche*), instead. Burlap or gunnysack wrapped around my high top shoes and secured with baling wire worked like magic; your shoes and feet never got wet.
hijito	Term of endearment; best translated as "my dear son."
hojas de maíz	Corn husks used for making tamales; the thin and soft and virtually transparent ones were also used in rolling a cigarette.
hojelata	Though pronounced differently it is a composite word stemming from *hoja de lata* or *hojalata* which stands for tin.
horno	An outdoor adobe oven used for baking homemade bread and other delicacies such as *molletes*, that is, sweet rolls that resembled a small loaf of bread; my paternal grandmother baked *molletes* at Christmastime .
l'agua	Instead of *el agua* it is common to hear l'agua, thereby employing the article *la*; in the process the letter <u>a</u> of the article *la* disappears.
luminarios	Though called *luminarias* or *farolitos* in other parts of New Mexico, we in the Río Puerco valley referred to them as *luminarios* (bonfires).

manoplas	One piece wool hand-mittens; no fingers except for the thumb.
marrano	Besides marrano, people in my valley used *cochino* and *puerco*, but we never used *cerdo*, a more standard term in Spain and other Spanish-speaking countries.
masa	Dough or paste made from corn boiled in limewater and ground in a pumice stone called *metate* (see below).
matanza	Butchering of a hog, once upon a time an annual fall tradition in many Hispanic households—including mine—throughout New Mexico.
metate	A large oval-shaped grinding stone with a depression. Once popular in New Mexico, it was used to grind corn with a hand-held smooth stone (The *metate* is different in shape from the *molcajete* found in Mexico which has three small legs.).
Misa del Gallo	Literally Rooster's Mass (i.e., Midnight Mass); legend has it that a rooster crowed the night the Baby Jesus was born.
muncho	Many people throughout the Spanish-speaking world pronounce *mucho* as *muncho*. New Mexico and the American Southwest are no exception.
nixtamal	Corn boiled in limewater; its *masa*, dough or paste, is used for making tamales.
Nochebuena	Literally the Good Night; it refers to Christmas Eve in New Mexico, Spain and other Spanish-speaking countries.
ocote	A term that comes from Náhuatal and means pitch or torch pine; it was used to fast start a fire above all the *luminarios*.
pa	*Para* is shortened to pa virtually every place where Spanish is spoken.
pantera	In New Mexico this term means elegant or dapper rather than brave, a more universal usage.
pichel	A word used for pitcher to hold water; once common in New Mexico. Some people may think it comes from the English pitcher, but pichel is heard in Mexico (e. g., Sinaloa and Sonora).
placita	Placita is the diminutive of plaza; in the story it means village.
quemoso	This word denotes something hot or spicy instead of *picante*; it is still heard among Hispanics in New Mexico and the American Southwest.
ranchito	Diminutive for rancho, a small ranch.
tamal	A word that comes from the Aztec *tamalli*; tamale is also popular in the Southwest regardless of ethnicity.
torta de pan	In immediate and extended families such as mine, a *torta de pan* was a loaf of bread.
trastero	The word comes from *trastes* for dishes; they were kept in a modest cupboard (*trastero*) made of pine wood.
viga	Round wooden beams were once visible in Hispanic homes; today they are a luxury item affordable only by people with money.

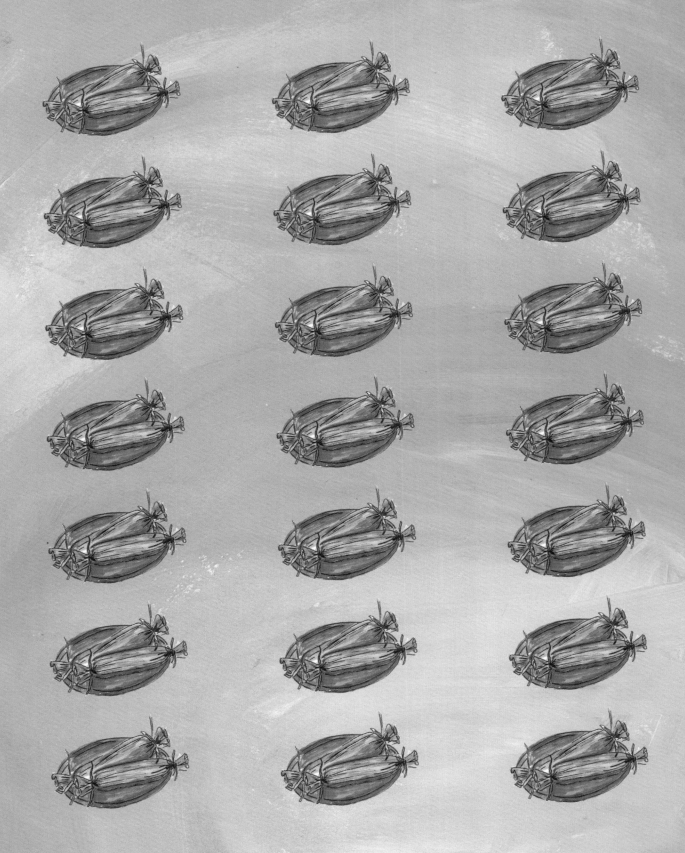

CPSIA information can be obtained
at www.ICGtesting.com
Printed in the USA
LVIC04*1030030815
448593LV00013B/30